The Busy Mom

by

Sharon Murphy Yates

Illustrated by Joan C. Waites

Child & Family Press ▪ Washington, DC

The Busy Mom

by

Sharon Murphy Yates

Illustrated by Joan C. Waites

Child & Family Press ▪ Washington, DC

Child & Family Press is an imprint of the Child Welfare League of America. The Child Welfare League of America is the nation's oldest and largest membership-based child welfare organization. We are committed to engaging people everywhere in promoting the well-being of children, youth, and their families, and protecting every child from harm.

CHILD WELFARE LEAGUE OF AMERICA, INC.

HEADQUARTERS

440 First Street NW, Third Floor

Washington, DC 20001-2085

E-mail: books@cwla.org

CURRENT PRINTING (last digit)

10 9 8 7 6 5 4 3 2 1

Cover and text design by James D. Melvin

Printed in the United States of America

LIBRARY OF CONGRESS CATALOGING-IN-PUBLICATION DATA

Yates, Sharon Murphy.
        The busy mom / Sharon Murphy Yates.
                p. cm.
Summary: As she rushes to get her little boy into bed, a busy mother realizes how precious her time with him is and tells him just how special he is to her.
ISBN 0-87868-789-0
[1. Mothers and sons--Fiction. 2. Bedtime--Fiction.] I. Title. II. Waites, Joan C., Ill.

PZ7.Y278 Bu 2001
(E)--dc21

                                                                99-046419

To James Steven Yates, Jr.,
my greatest gift to the world...a work in progress.
—S.M.Y.

To My Family.

—J.C.W.

It's time for bed,
His mother said...

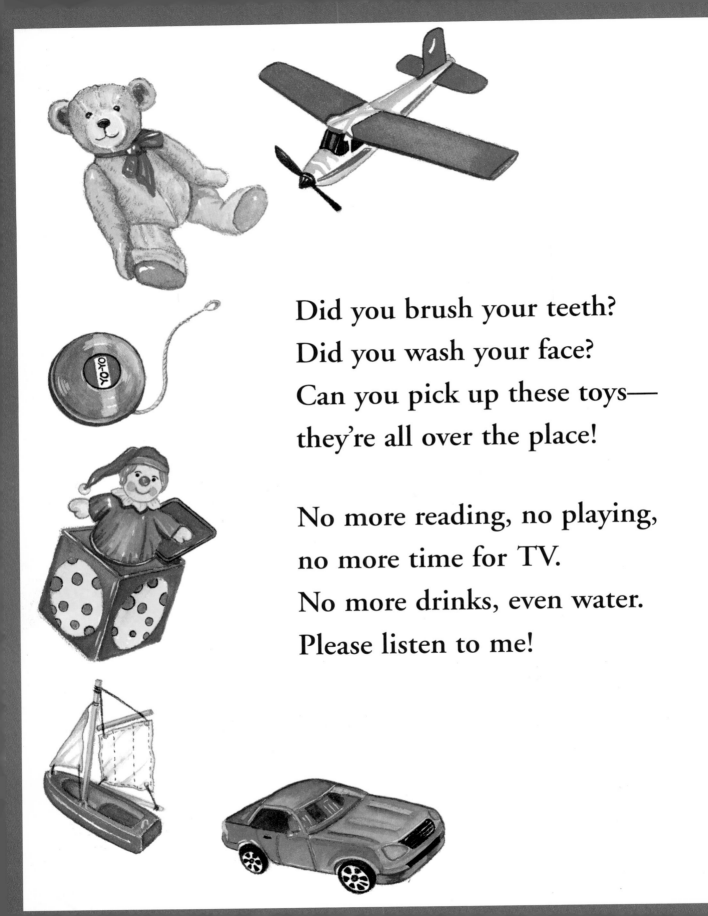

Did you brush your teeth?
Did you wash your face?
Can you pick up these toys—
they're all over the place!

No more reading, no playing,
no more time for TV.
No more drinks, even water.
Please listen to me!

You need what for tomorrow?!
Why didn't you tell me before?
And what have I told you
about these things on the floor?

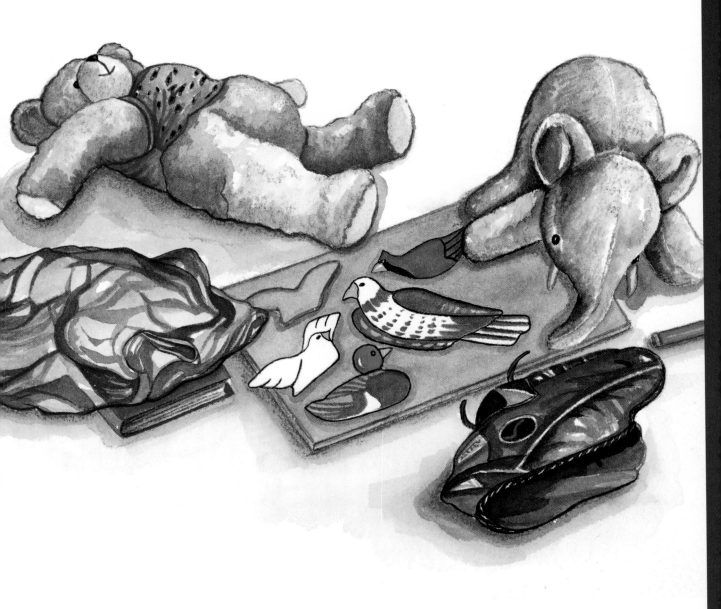

It's late and you're tired...
and I'm tired too...
and I've got so much stuff
that I've still got to do.

Stop stalling. Come on now.
It's been a long day.
Get back in your bed.
Go to sleep right away!

Then she quickly said, "Love you!"
to go on her way,
her mind full of things
to do for the next day.

She turned to her son
for one last good night,
but just as she started
to turn out the light...

She looked at him there,
all sprawled out on his bed,
with feet sticking out
and bears by his head...

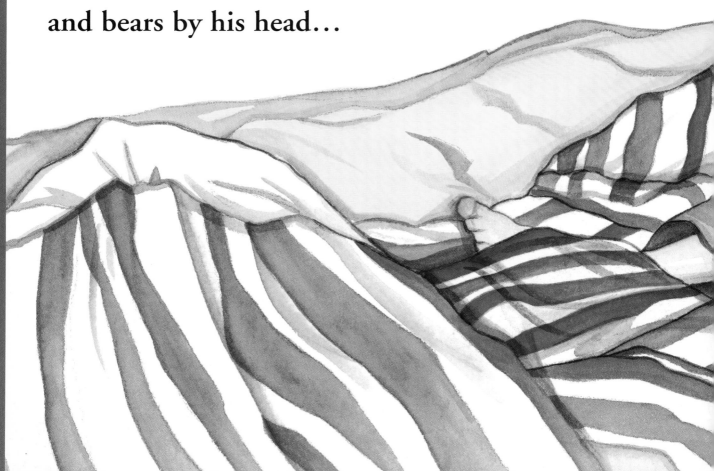

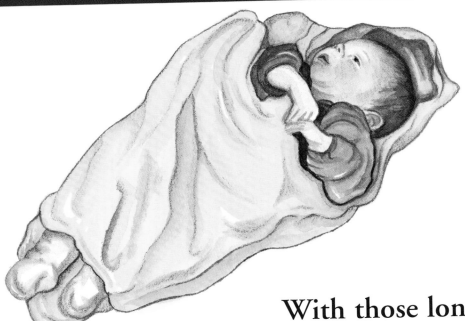

With those long lanky legs,
the world's sweetest face,
growing up so quickly
that time seemed to race.

And she thought as she stood there
and looked at her son,
how happy he'd made her
since his life had begun.

And wasn't it yesterday
that he was so small?
But look at him now—
he's growing so tall.

Where did the time go?
How did I lose track
of those moments I've lost
that I'll never get back?

She stopped and she turned…
and she went to his bed,
and she sat down beside him
and smiled as she said,

Sometimes I get busy
and I don't always say
how much I love you
and how every day...

I think of how lucky I am
in so many ways,
to have you to share
all my love and my days.

You're smart and you're funny,
you're clever and kind,
and you're all of those things
that I had in mind
when I dreamed of the boy
who would someday be mine.

I love to watch you playing.
I love to hold your hand.
I love the things you draw for me,
the adventures you have planned.

I love it when you're silly.
I love to hear you sing.
I love the times when there's just us,
the fun that those times bring.

I love to see that funny dance
that no one else can do.
I love your stories. I love your smile.
I love your face. I LOVE YOU!

So forgive me when it seems like
I don't have time for you,
and when there are so many
other things I have to do.
Remember, dear, my favorite times
will always be with you!

Then she hugged him and kissed him
and hugged him again,
and tucked him in sweetly,
turned the light out, and then...

She stayed a while longer
and standing right there,
she took a few moments
to say a short prayer.

Of thanks for her treasure,
A gift from above,
Her child, her greatest joy in life—
The one she'll always love!

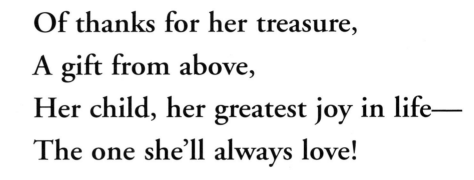